YORK NOTES

Tess of the d'Urbervilles

Thomas Hardy

Notes by David Langston

Longman   York Press

YORK PRESS
322 Old Brompton Road, London SW5 9JH

Pearson Education Limited
Edinburgh Gate, Harlow,
Essex CM20 2JE, United Kingdom
Associated companies, branches and representatives throughout the world

© Librairie du Liban *Publishers* and Addison Wesley Longman Limited 1998

First published 1998
Second impression 1999

ISBN 0-582-36841-3

Designed by Vicki Pacey, Trojan Horse, London
Illustrations by Jenny Bidgood
Map by Gay Galsworthy
Phototypeset by Gem Graphics, Trenance, Mawgan Porth, Cornwall
Colour reproduction and film output by Spectrum Colour
Produced by Addison Wesley Longman China Limited, Hong Kong

CONTENTS

Preface   **4**

PART ONE

INTRODUCTION   How to Study a Novel   **5**
                Thomas Hardy's Background   **6**
                Context & Setting   **8**

PART TWO

SUMMARIES   General Summary   **11**
                Tess Durbeyfield's Country   **12**
                Detailed Summaries, Comment,
                    Glossaries & Tests   **15**
                    Chapters 1–24   **15**
                    Chapters 25–44   **32**
                    Chapters 45–59   **45**

PART THREE

COMMENTARY   Themes   **54**
                Structure   **58**
                Characters   **59**
                Language & Style   **63**

PART FOUR

STUDY SKILLS   How to Use Quotations   **70**
                Essay Writing   **67**
                Sample Essay Plan & Questions   **70**
                Further Questions   **71**

PART FIVE

CULTURAL CONNECTIONS
                Broader Perspectives   **73**
Literary Terms   **75**
Test Answers   **76**

PREFACE

York Notes are designed to give you a broader perspective on works of literature studied at GCSE and equivalent levels. We have carried out extensive research into the needs of the modern literature student prior to publishing this new edition. Our research showed that no existing series fully met students' requirements. Rather than present a single authoritative approach, we have provided alternative viewpoints, empowering students to reach their own interpretations of the text. York Notes provide a close examination of the work and include biographical and historical background, summaries, glossaries, analyses of characters, themes, structure and language, cultural connections and literary terms.

If you look at the Contents page you will see the structure for the series. However, there's no need to read from the beginning to the end as you would with a novel, play, poem or short story. Use the Notes in the way that suits you. Our aim is to help you with your understanding of the work, not to dictate how you should learn.

York Notes are written by English teachers and examiners, with an expert knowledge of the subject. They show you how to succeed in coursework and examination assignments, guiding you through the text and offering practical advice. Questions and comments will extend, test and reinforce your knowledge. Attractive colour design and illustrations improve clarity and understanding, making these Notes easy to use and handy for quick reference.

York Notes are ideal for:
• Essay writing
• Exam preparation
• Class discussion

David Langston MA is a part-time lecturer in Adult Education, former Head of English and an examiner at GCSE level for a major examination board. He has written and contributed to GCSE textbooks.

The text used in these Notes is the new Penguin Classics edition, published 1996, edited by Michael Mason.

Health Warning: **This study guide will enhance your understanding, but should not replace the reading of the original text and/or study in class.**

PART ONE

INTRODUCTION

HOW TO STUDY A NOVEL

You have bought this book because you wanted to study a novel on your own. This may supplement classwork.

- You will need to read the novel several times. Start by reading it quickly for pleasure, then read it slowly and carefully. Further readings will generate new ideas and help you to memorise the details of the story.
- Make careful notes on themes, plot and characters of the novel. The plot will change some of the characters. Who changes?
- The novel may not present events chronologically. Does the novel you are reading begin at the beginning of the story or does it contain flashbacks and a muddled time sequence? Can you think why?
- How is the story told? Is it narrated by one of the characters or by an all-seeing ('omniscient') narrator?
- Does the same person tell the story all the way through? Or do we see the events through the minds and feelings of a number of different people.
- Which characters does the narrator like? Which characters do you like or dislike? Do your sympathies change during the course of the book? Why? When?
- Any piece of writing (including your notes and essays) is the result of thousands of choices. No book had to be written in just one way: the author could have chosen other words, other phrases, other characters, other events. How could the author of your novel have written the story differently? If events were recounted by a minor character how would this change the novel?

Studying on your own requires self-discipline and a carefully thought-out work plan in order to be effective. Good luck.

The Hardy Family

Thomas Hardy was born on 2 June 1840 in Higher Bockhampton, a small village near Dorchester in the county of Dorset. The area of southwest England where he grew up was to provide a setting for several of his major novels. Thomas's father, a master mason and building contractor, played the violin and passed on his love of music to his son. From his mother he acquired an enthusiasm for reading.

The Hardys had once owned land and there had been some prominent figures in the family. One of them, Admiral Hardy, had been with Nelson when he was killed at the battle of Trafalgar.

Thomas was conscious that his family had known grander days and later in life he felt that the Hardys were fated to die out. We can perhaps find echoes of these feelings in the decline of the d'Urbervilles.

Childhood

Thomas was a weak child and was kept at home until he was eight, but he could read at an early age. He eventually went to school in Dorchester where he was regarded as an outstanding scholar but also as a solitary and sensitive boy who avoided company. As a youth he witnessed two public hangings in Dorchester which had deep and long-lasting effects on him. One of those executed was a woman who had murdered her lover. It is likely that this event provided some material for the story of Tess.

Architecture

After leaving school Thomas was taken on as a pupil by a Dorchester architect. Six years later, in 1862, he moved to work for a firm in London. He had read widely and by this time had begun to write poetry.

In London he continued with his self-education in his spare time, reading and visiting galleries and museums. His first novel, 'The Poor Man and the Lady', was begun in 1867. Although this book was rejected by publishers as being too political and biased against the upper class, Hardy continued to write.

Success and marriage

In 1870 Hardy was sent by his firm to St Juliot's in north Cornwall to estimate the cost of repairs to the church. There he met Emma Gifford, the twenty-nine-year-old sister-in-law of the clergyman. Over a period of four years he visited St Juliot's several times on business and he and Emma wrote to each other.

Desperate Remedies, a murder mystery, was published in 1871 with moderate success and *Under the Greenwood Tree* followed in 1872.

Far from the Madding Crowd (1874), which, like *Tess of the d'Urbervilles*, centres on a female character, marked the beginning of Hardy's full-time career as a writer and he felt successful enough to marry Emma Gifford.

Hardy's most popular and highly regarded novels dealt with life in his native countryside. *The Return of the Native* (1878) and *The Mayor of Casterbridge* (1886) were, like *Far from the Madding Crowd*, set in Wessex, the old Saxon name he used for the southwest of England.

When *Tess of the d'Urbervilles* was published in 1891 it was a great success but it also provoked a storm of protest about what was seen to be its immoral content. *Jude the Obscure* (1895) caused even more controversy and Hardy gave up writing fiction and turned back to his first love, poetry. He preferred to be thought of as a poet who had written some novels.

Religion

Religion played an important part in Hardy's childhood and throughout his life he had a love of churches and church music. As a young man he began to have religious doubts and, looking at the cruelties and suffering in the world around him, like Angel Clare in

Tess of the d'Urbervilles, he found it hard to believe in a kind and loving God. However, just as his heroine Tess suggests in Chapter 47 (p. 410), he thought that it was left to human beings to fill this gap and to treat each other with 'loving kindness'.

Old age   The death of Emma in 1912 prompted Hardy to write some of his most moving poetry.

In 1914 he married Florence Dugdale who had worked as his secretary. He continued to write in his old age and was visited by many famous writers at his home, Max Gate. Hardy died in 1928 and was given a grand funeral in Westminster Abbey, but his heart was buried with his family in Stinsford churchyard.

Context & setting

Thomas Hardy lived through most of the reign of Queen Victoria and well into the twentieth century, years which saw great changes in industry, science and society. In his lifetime the British Empire expanded and along with it grew Britain's domination of world trade.

Hardy had been brought up on tales of the Napoleonic Wars and was alive during the Crimean, the Boer, and the First World wars. These examples of man's tendency to revert to savagery in order to resolve disagreements contributed to his doubts about the existence of a loving God.

Life in the countryside

After 1846 British farmers were no longer protected against the importation of foreign corn. This resulted in considerable changes in agriculture. Many farmers took to raising sheep and cattle which were more profitable than growing corn and required fewer workers.

Large-scale farming for profit and the introduction of machinery increased the use of seasonal labour. Workers moved from place to place and the old traditions and customs were weakened as well as the old ties between farmer and worker. We see two aspects of this large-scale farming in the novel. The working environment at Talbothays is pleasant: however, it is seasonal employment, whereas at Flintcomb-Ash Tess experiences sheer repetitive drudgery toiling in the fields and feeding the machines.

Changes in farming affected peasant families like the Durberfields.

This process also saw the end of the small independent peasant class, those people who lived by necessary trades or as small dealers or carriers, such as Tess's father. They were often tenants of smallholdings and when their leases ran out these were swallowed up by the large farming businesses. The dispossessed peasants then joined the bottom layer of landless labourers or, like thousands of others, moved to seek work in the industrial towns. Many emigrated in search of a better life.

THE POPULAR NOVEL

As the nineteenth century progressed and more people were learning to read, there was a growing demand for stories published in a form which the average person could afford. Novels were first serialised in weekly or monthly magazines which often had very large circulations, before they were published as books. Writers could make their fortunes in this way. Charles Dickens was one of the most successful writers in this form. *Tess of the d'Urbervilles* was first published in this manner.

Religion & ideas

Religion was taken very seriously in Victorian times but by the middle of the nineteenth century some educated people were expressing doubts about the literal truth of the Bible. Charles Darwin's *On the Origin of Species* (1859) offered a theory of the evolution of life which was incompatible with the account of creation in the Book of Genesis.

Many, like Hardy, became agnostic, feeling that it was impossible to know whether there was a God or not and that there was no reason to believe that good would triumph over evil in the world.

Hardy offended Victorian notions of morality. Middle-class society, however, continued to hold to a strict moral code, particularly regarding sexual behaviour. *Tess of the d'Urbervilles* was denounced as immoral because of its content, as was *Jude the Obscure*.

Hardy tried to deal with issues which everyone knew about but few were willing to discuss openly and he felt that it was a hopeful sign that many readers were willing to accept novels which did not have conventional, morally correct endings.

PART TWO

SUMMARIES

GENERAL SUMMARY

Chapters 1–24 John Durbeyfield, a haggler or carrier, is told by a local
Phase the first clergyman that he is descended from an ancient noble
– 'The maiden' family, the d'Urbervilles. When his horse, his main
and Phase the source of income, is killed, he and his wife persuade
second – their daughter Tess to go and claim kinship with the
'Maiden no newly rich Stoke-d'Urbervilles, a family who have no
more' real claim to the name.

Tess is employed to look after the fowls belonging
to the blind Mrs d'Urberville. She is seduced by
the dissolute son, Alec, and returns home to
Marlott where she gives birth to a child which soon
dies.

Phase the Two years later, Tess, wishing to make a fresh start,
third – 'The goes to work for the summer season on a dairy farm
rally' some miles to the south. The work is pleasant and the
company congenial. Angel Clare, the son of a
clergyman, is working at the farm. To his father's
great disappointment he has rejected a career in the
Church. He is learning the dairy business with a
view to emigrating and farming abroad. Tess and
Angel grow very fond of each other. He thinks
she will make an ideal farmer's wife. Tess feels that she
should be honest with Angel about her past but takes
her mother's advice to say nothing. After overcoming
her doubts, Tess agrees to marry him.

On their wedding night, Angel confesses to having
committed an immoral act in his past and Tess takes
this opportunity to tell him about her seduction by Alec
d'Urberville and its result.

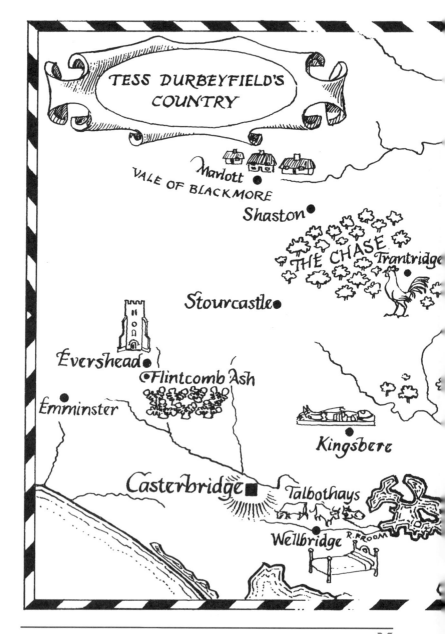

Chapters 25–44
Phase the fourth – 'The consequence' and Phase the fifth – 'The woman pays'

Angel's image of Tess as an unspoiled country girl is destroyed. He leaves her and eventually travels to Brazil.

Tess goes to work on a farm at Flintcomb-Ash where the farmer is a bully, conditions are harsh and the labour is exhausting. One Sunday, anxious for some news of her husband, she decides to walk to the home of Angel's parents but when she arrives she is unable to summon up the courage to make herself known.

Chapters 45–59
Phase the sixth – 'The convert'

Tess finds herself once again pursued by Alec d'Urberville. He has undergone a religious conversion and is travelling the countryside as a preacher. His obsession with Tess causes him to abandon his religion and he insists that he has a greater claim on her than her husband.

Tess's father dies and her family are soon homeless. They take temporary shelter in the church which contains the ancient family vaults of the d'Urbervilles. Alec offers to help them.

Phase the seventh – 'Fulfilment'

Angel Clare returns from Brazil and looks for Tess. He finds her living in Sandbourne as Alec d'Urberville's wife. She feels that it is too late to retrieve their marriage and she sends him away but in her anger and despair she kills Alec and follows her husband. She enjoys a brief period of happiness with Angel, spending a night with him in an empty house. However, she is arrested at Stonehenge the following night and is later hanged at Wintoncester. Angel, with Tess's blessing, leaves with her young sister.

Chapters 1–24

Phase the first – 'the maiden'

Chapters 1–3 (Sir John)

One evening, John Durbeyfield, a small dealer and carrier, is walking home to the village of Marlott. He meets Parson Tringham, a local clergyman and amateur historian who tells him that he is descended from the noble family of d'Urbervilles who used to own great estates, and that his ancestors are buried in marble tombs at Kingsbere.

The parson knows that his news is of no practical use.

The parson wonders whether he has been wise in giving him this information.

Durbeyfield decides he must behave according to his new-found status and sends for a carriage to take him home.

The ancient country customs have not quite died out in Marlott.

The village of Marlott lies in the green sheltered valley of Blackmoor. The women of the village are taking part in an ancient custom of parading round the village in white dresses. As they are about to enter a field where they will dance, John Durbeyfield appears seated in the back of a carriage, drunkenly boasting about his ancestors. One of the group of women is John's daughter Tess, a girl of sixteen, who is extremely embarrassed by her father's behaviour.

This chance meeting is rather poignant in the light of later events.

The women proceed to dance in the meadow and are observed by three young middle-class men who are on a walking holiday. They are brothers and one of them, Angel, stays to join in the dance as the others walk on. When he leaves he notices Tess and wishes he had chosen her as his partner.

The young man has made an impression on Tess and it is some time before she returns to the dancing.

However, she is concerned about her father's strange behaviour and she leaves early. She arrives home to find her mother in the midst of children and washing but full of excitement about her husband's news. She also tells Tess that he has been told by the doctor that he has a heart complaint.

Mrs Durbeyfield leaves Tess in charge of the children while she goes to fetch her husband from the pub. This is also an excuse to spend a little time there herself as it is one of the few pleasures in her hard life.

After some time Tess sends her young brother to fetch her parents as she knows that her father has to set off soon after midnight to transport a load of beehives. Eventually she has to go to the pub herself.

COMMENT   The parson's careless remarks make a deep impression. History is merely a hobby to him.

Our first view of Tess is as an innocent and sensitive girl. She is embarrassed by her father but tries to make excuses for him.

We are given a brief introduction to Angel Clare who is an important character later in the story.

Tess is aware of the shortcomings of her home and her parents' disorganised way of life.

Mrs Durbeyfield is a simple and superstitious woman and represents the old peasant culture. Tess has had some education and thinks more rationally.

Tess can speak in both **dialect** (see Literary Terms) and in a more standard form of English.

GLOSSARY   **haggler**   a small trader or carrier

black-pot   black pudding, a sausage made with boiled blood

chitterlings   pigs' intestines

vamp   walk or tramp

fess   lively

mommet   a puppet or dressed-up doll

larry   commotion, disturbance

plim   swell up

vlee   a fly, a type of small carriage

mampus   a crowd

rafted   shocked, disturbed

CHAPTERS 4—6 (NEW RELATIONS)

Mrs Durbeyfield, having joined her husband at Rolliver's, tells him of her plan to send Tess to visit a rich lady called d'Urberville. She believes that this woman is likely to be a relative and that the meeting can only do Tess some good. It could even lead to Tess finding a wealthy husband.

It is ironic that Tess thinks of herself as a murderess (see Chapter 56).

When Tess arrives the family return home.

At two in the morning Durbeyfield is in no state to go to market so Tess sets out with young Abraham for company. They both fall asleep and their horse is killed when they collide with the mail cart. Tess feels like a murderess and that she is personally responsible for ruining the family business which has depended heavily on the horse.

PHASE THE FIRST – 'THE MAIDEN'

Tess's mother is able to persuade her to go and make herself known to the wealthy Mrs d'Urberville. This family is in no way related to the Durbeyfields. Their name is one which they had adopted when, after having made a fortune in industry, they had decided to buy a country estate and live as landed gentry.

The d'Urberville's house is new, like their adopted name.

When Tess arrives at the d'Urberville house, she is surprised to find everything looking so neat and new. She is met by Alec, Mrs d'Urberville's son, who explains that his mother is an invalid and is unable to receive her. Tess, feeling embarrassed, explains why she has come. Alec, who finds her very attractive, gives her food and says he will get his mother to provide her with a position.

We share Tess's unease about Alec's part in the job offer.

Tess arrives home the following day to find that a letter has been delivered which contains the offer of a job looking after Mrs d'Urberville's poultry. She is reluctant to leave home and searches unsuccessfully for local work. One day when she is out Alec calls at the house and asks if Tess will accept the position. Tess reluctantly decides to go.

COMMENT

Tess feels that she is responsible for the death of the horse and must find work to help support the family.

Her mother has dreams of Tess finding a wealthy husband. She imagines that difference in social class will be no problem now that the Durbeyfields have discovered their noble ancestry.

Hardy contrasts the new d'Urberville estate with the ancient woodland nearby.

We see that Tess is sensitive and proud. She is reluctant to go seeking favours from dubious relatives, and she has no wish to change her social position.

Tess approaches things in a practical and sensible way. Unlike her mother she sees the offer of work merely as a chance to help the family by earning some money.

GLOSSARY   **cwoffer** coffer, a wooden chest

gaffer a foreman, official

projick project, scheme

sumple supple

get green malt in floor become pregnant

eastings turning to the east during church services

nater nature

stubbard-tree a variety of apple tree

knacker horse-slaughterer

good-now (dialect) you may believe it

Malthusian Thomas Malthus (1766–1834), an economist who believed that unchecked population growth would bring about disaster

crumby (slang) delicious

dolorifuge something to help get rid of sorrow

fairlings fairings, presents or trinkets won or bought at a fair

spring cart a light carriage with spring suspension

CHAPTERS 7—9 (LEAVING HOME)

Tess is dressed in virginal white when she leaves home.

On the morning of her departure Tess is persuaded by her mother to wash her hair and wear her white dress. She is sad to leave her family but is irritated by her mother's belief that Mrs d'Urberville's son Alec has taken a fancy to her and intends to marry her.

Durbeyfield tells his daughter to pass on the message that he will sell the title to the d'Urbervilles, eventually reducing the price from £1,000 to £20.

Alec d'Urberville comes to meet Tess in a smart light carriage. She would rather have travelled in the cart with her box but she reluctantly accepts his offer of a lift. Her mother and the young children are sad to see her go and later Mrs Durbeyfield expresses her doubts to her husband.

Tess is still affected by the death of the family's horse.

During the journey Alec takes pleasure in frightening Tess by driving down hills at speed. He is encouraged in this behaviour when Tess holds onto his waist in fear. He persuades her to let him kiss her but is offended when she wipes her face. After deliberately losing her hat and jumping down to retrieve it, Tess refuses to get back into the carriage and walks the rest of the way to Tantridge with Alec driving alongside her.

Tess begins working at the d'Urberville's, looking after the hens and ornamental fowls, housed in an abandoned cottage. In the morning she is required to present the fowls for Mrs d'Urberville's inspection and is surprised to find that Alec's mother is blind. Mrs d'Urberville wants Tess to whistle to her bullfinches and Alec helps her to learn. He keeps his distance, however, and she becomes more used to him.

Alec is more cautious in his treatment of Tess.

COMMENT

We see that Alec is a bully who is used to having his own way. He is angry when Tess resists him, and outsmarts him.

Mrs d'Urberville's fowls are housed in a cottage once occupied by a peasant family whose lease had run out. Tess's family is later made homeless in this way (see Chapter 51).

The d'Urberville estate is not a productive one. It is merely an elegant residence and Tess's work is to look after Mrs d'Urberville's hobby.

GLOSSARY   **dand** (dialect) smart or stylish

                      lammicken (dialect) clumsy

                      gig or dog-cart types of light carriage

                      buck lively young man

                      holmberry holly berry

                      copyholders tenants whose rights were written in the 'copy' of the manor roll. The tenancy was often limited to a certain number of generations

                      out of her books (dialect) out of favour

CHAPTERS 10–11 (THE CHASE)

It seems that Alec is almost stalking Tess.

Tess is persuaded to join the other estate workers in visiting a local town on Saturday evenings. On one such outing she arrives late and finds her friends at a dance. Alec arrives and offers her a lift home but she is still wary of him and decides to wait for the others.

'Out of the frying-pan into the fire!'

As they are walking home a row breaks out and one of the women accuses Tess of laughing at her and challenges her to fight. Alec arrives at this moment and Tess accepts a lift on the back of his horse. Some of the women laugh as if they know what will happen.

Tess is confused and disarmed by Alec's generosity to her family.

They ride along and Alec complains to Tess about her resistance to his advances. She realises they have gone out of their way and accuses him of treachery. Alec tells her he has sent gifts to her family, including a horse. They are in The Chase, an ancient forest. He agrees to guide her or take her home but leaves her with his horse while he goes to look for directions. When he returns he finds Tess asleep. This is when the seduction or rape takes place.

COMMENT   Tess is really an onlooker at the Saturday night outings. She does not join in the drinking and dancing.

Hardy's references to Classical mythology refer to tales of sexual passion and prepare us for what happens in The Chase.

Because of the conventions of his time, Hardy was unable to describe what happened between Alec and Tess at the end of Chapter 11.

Hardy offers the possibilities that what happened to Tess was ordained by fate or that it may have been retribution for some ancient sins committed by her noble ancestors.

GLOSSARY   **parish relief** local welfare payments in money or food

Pan Greek god of nature, goatlike and lecherous

Syrinxes Syrinx was a nymph pursued by Pan

Priapus god of fertility and sexuality

Lotis daughter of the sea god, pursued by Priapus

Sileni gods of the forest who were usually drunk

jints (dialect) joints

Praxitelean like the work of Praxiteles, a Greek sculptor

cob a short-legged, strong horse

PHASE THE SECOND – 'MAIDEN NO MORE'

CHAPTERS 12–13 (TESS GOES HOME)

Alec admits he is bad and is likely to remain so.

A few weeks later Tess is on her way home. She accepts a lift from Alec but resists his pleas to change her mind about leaving. Later she walks part of the way with a man who is painting religious texts on stiles and walls.

He mentions a clergyman called Clare who is to preach in the neighbourhood.

When she arrives home Tess tells her mother that she is pregnant. Her mother accepts the pregnancy as a natural occurrence but is angry and disappointed that she has not managed to get Alec to marry her.

Apart from one visit to church, when she feels she is the object of gossip, Tess avoids company and walks alone in the evenings feeling guilty about her condition.

COMMENT   Alec tempts Tess with the life of a 'kept woman'. Marriage is not mentioned.

The man with the pot of paint represents the narrow literal view of the Bible which was common among religious people at the time.

Mrs Durbeyfield shows an old-fashioned peasant attitude in her acceptance of Tess's pregnancy but she has no understanding of the social divide which made a marriage between Tess and Alec extremely improbable in the first place.

Hardy gives us an unfavourable view of the churchgoers as they appear to gossip about Tess.

GLOSSARY   **barked-oak twigs** twigs which have had the bark stripped off
teave (dialect) struggle
hontish (dialect) haughty, proud
Robert South a famous preacher (1634–1716)
lumber furniture and other items stored and out of use
Langdon a hymn tune named after its composer

CHAPTERS 14–15 (SORROW)

Tess struggles against her feelings but dearly loves the baby.

By harvesttime in August Tess has had the baby and is working in the fields. She has rejoined the life of the village and has the sympathy of her fellow workers as they observe her nursing her child. It is rumoured among them that she was raped.

Durbeyfield's foolish pride makes him refuse to let Tess send for the vicar.

Tess's baby is taken ill. When she fears he is going to die she wants to have him baptised but her father will not allow her to send for the vicar. In the night, with the help of the other children, she baptises him Sorrow. The baby dies in the early morning.

The following evening Tess goes to see the parson and he is sympathetic enough to assure her that her baptism of the child was valid. However, he refuses to give him a Christian burial. She tells the vicar she will never enter his church again. The baby is buried at night in a corner of the churchyard and Tess secretly places a homemade cross on the grave.

Tess has survived her experiences and gained self-knowledge.

Tess remains at home, helping with various domestic tasks and thinking about her experiences. She has matured and she begins to look to the future, hoping to find a new start. She does not feel comfortable in Marlott, and one spring, between two and three years after her return from Tantridge, she decides to take up a job as a dairymaid at Talbothays some distance away.

COMMENT

Hardy opens Chapter 14 as a distant and rather detached observer and only gradually comes to focus on Tess. She is part of the autumnal harvest scene.

The church is once again presented in a poor light when the vicar refuses Sorrow a Christian burial.

The baptism and burial of Sorrow are particularly moving. We are reminded that Tess is little more than a child herself.

When Tess thinks over her life and her recent experiences we see that she has gained enough confidence firmly to reject her mother's fantasies about their noble ancestry.

GLOSSARY   **heliolatries** sun worship

shock a group of corn-sheaves leant against each other

Aholah and Aholibah biblical harlots, sinful women

stopt-diapason one of the sounds produced by a church-organ

Roger Ascham scholar and teacher (1515–68). This is from *The Schoolmaster* (1570)

Jeremy Taylor religious writer (1613–67)

PHASE THE THIRD – 'THE RALLY'

CHAPTERS $16-18$ (THE MILKMAID AND ANGEL CLARE)

Tess feels optimistic as she enters the Valley of the Great Dairies.

Tess sets out for her new job on a fine May morning. She travels through Stourcastle, and later comes within sight of Kingsbere, where her ancestors are buried. She mentally rejects their importance, and then travels by foot over Egdon Heath. Eventually she reaches the Valley of the Great Dairies where Talbothays is situated. This is an area of large-scale farming where workers are employed seasonally (see Context & Setting). She hears the cows being called in for milking and follows them to the farm.

Tess is relieved when Angel does not recognise her.

Mr Crick, the dairyman, welcomes Tess to the farm and she joins in the milking right away. When the cows seem reluctant to yield milk, someone suggests singing to them and the men and women milkers join in. It is then suggested that one of the milkers should play his harp. Tess is curious that the dairyman should address this man as 'sir' and then she recognises him as the young stranger who had joined in the club-dance at Marlott. Angel Clare is the son of a parson and he is studying farming methods.

Angel feels free to read and think as he likes.

We learn that Angel is youngest of three brothers and that he has disappointed his father by rejecting the Church as a career, finding it impossible to accept certain doctrines of the Church of England (see Context & Setting, also Thomas Hardy's Background).

He has come to appreciate the qualities of the country people and to enjoy the outdoor life. Angel finds Tess attractive and has a feeling that he has seen her before.

COMMENT   Tess's cheerful state of mind is in tune with the pleasant and fertile scene in the valley.

The atmosphere at milking time is friendly but businesslike. This is a working farm, unlike the d'Urberville estate.

This is the beginning of a happy period in Tess's life.

Hardy indicates his dislike of the **stereotype** (see Literary Terms) of Hodge, the popular image of the stupid countryman. Through Angel he suggests beneficial effects of close contact with nature and the seasons.

It is sadly **ironic** (see Literary Terms) that Angel admires Tess as being 'fresh and virginal'. This foreshadows his response when she tells him of her history.

GLOSSARY   **Van Asloot, Salleart** Flemish painters

steading farm buildings

barton farmyard

milchers milk-cows

Olympian like the Greek gods who lived on Mount Olympus

pattens wooden overshoes

pinner (dialect) apron

cowcumber (dialect) cucumber

kex dry hollow stalks

nott (dialect) hornless

William Dewey a character in *Under the Greenwood Tree* by Thomas Hardy

tranter casual carrier of goods

leery empty, hungry

leads milk pans made of lead

Low Church Evangelical tendency in the Church of England, against ornament and excessive ritual

High (Church) tendency in the Church of England nearest to
  Roman Catholicism

wrings cheese presses

thimble riggers cheats, con-men

Hodge common **stereotype** (see Literary Terms) of the
  countryman

Pascal French philosopher (1632–62)

mess dine, eat together

CHAPTERS 19–21 (MUTUAL ATTRACTION)

Angel despises old noble families.

One evening Tess hears Angel playing his harp. He
finds her in the garden and talks to her. He is surprised
by her pessimistic outlook on life. Later she fears that
she has made a poor impression and wonders if she
should tell him about her noble ancestry. This idea is
put out of her head by dairyman Crick when he tells
her that Angel Clare has no time for old families.

Tess falls into the routine of the dairy and is happier
than she has been for some time. She and Angel are
early risers and find themselves working together in the
dawn. In the dim light Angel feels that Tess is like a
representative of all women, like a goddess. They are on
the verge of falling in love.

The old superstitions have not died out.

One morning there is great concern in the dairy
because the butter will not set in the churn. Dairyman
Crick is considering calling in the help of a conjuror or
wise-man as it is generally believed that this problem is
caused by some supernatural affliction. Someone
mentions a superstition that it can be caused by the
presence of a person in love. This prompts dairyman
Crick to tell a story about an ex-employee who had
hidden in the churn to avoid the angry mother of his
pregnant girlfriend. Tess feels faint at this point and
goes outside for some air. Soon the butter starts to form
in the churn.

In the evening Tess overhears some of the other girls talking of how they are in love with Angel but, according to one of them, he is in love with Tess. They doubt that a gentleman like him would marry any of them anyway. Tess feels it would not be right to let any man marry her.

COMMENT   We see that Tess has had some education when she talks to Angel in the garden. He is intrigued when he finds that she also casts doubts on conventional beliefs.

Tess is aware that social class may be a barrier between them and she is tempted to tell Angel about her ancestors.

In the early morning scene Hardy is letting us see something of how Angel views Tess.

Tess is saddened by the story which is a reminder of her own seduction.

GLOSSARY   **cuckoo-spittle** frothy secretion on plants made by an insect

apple-blooth (dialect) apple-blossom

hobble (dialect) problem

Valley of Humiliation in John Bunyan's *Pilgrim's Progress*

man of Uz Job in the Old Testament

niaiseries (French) silliness

rozum (dialect) nonsense, or a person with foolish ideas

convenances polite social customs

Artemis a Greek virgin goddess, a huntress

Demeter Greek goddess of agriculture

conjuror a wise-man who told fortunes and provided cures

cast folk's waters told fortunes by examining people's urine (not in all editions)

touchwood dry rotten wood

ballyragging verbally bullying or abusing

by side and by seam thoroughly

pummy the pulp left after apples are pressed for cider
dog-days hot days in late summer
zid (dialect) saw

CHAPTERS 22–4 (A DECLARATION)

Tess wants to be fair to the other girls and give them every chance with Angel.

The butter is spoiled by the cows having eaten wild garlic in a particular field. The workers all set out to clear the field of the weeds. Angel and Tess are working close together. She points out some of the other girls and suggests that any one of them would make him a good wife. She tells him not to think of marrying her. After this she tries to avoid him and to give the other girls a chance.

The girls are generous in their feelings about Angel's preference for Tess.

One Sunday morning, two months after her arrival at the dairy, Tess is going to church with three of the milkmaids when they find the road flooded. They are reluctant to wade through it because they are wearing their Sunday best and thin shoes. Angel comes along and carries each of the girls through the water. He tells Tess that he has carried the others so that he can carry her. The others say that it is obvious that Angel favours Tess. That night one of the girls tells Tess that she has heard that Angel's family have chosen a young lady of

his own class who they think would make him a
suitable wife.

In August the hot weather becomes oppressive and the
cows are milked in the fields. One day Angel is
watching Tess as she works and admiring her beauty.
Overcome by a combination of the heat of the day and
passion, he kneels beside her and clasps her in his arms,
declaring his love for her. Tess cries and eventually they
return to their milking.

COMMENT   Tess reasons that if Angel is looking for a wife then any
one of the other three girls will do as well as she.

The other girls do not really believe that Angel, being a
gentleman, will ever marry a milkmaid.

Hardy begins Chapter 24 with images of fertility and
ripeness before describing the heat and its effects,
finally moving in to focus on Angel and Tess.

GLOSSARY   **twang** a sharp unpleasant flavour

continny (dialect) continue

That-it-may-please-Thees words from church service

un-Sabbatarian not appropriate for the Sabbath (Sunday)

thistlespud a tool for digging up thistles

sermons in stones from *As You Like It* by William Shakespeare,
a reference to finding one's religion in Nature

paltered hesitated, avoided the issue

Thermidorean hot; Thermidor began on 19 July in the French
Revolutionary calendar

diurnal roll daily turning of the earth

aura (Latin) breeze

A *Identify the speaker.*

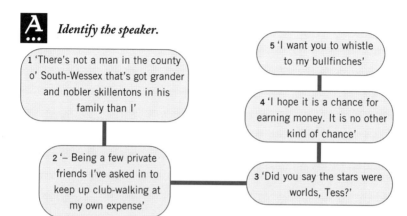

1 'There's not a man in the county o' South-Wessex that's got grander and nobler skillentons in his family than I'

2 '– Being a few private friends I've asked in to keep up club-walking at my own expense'

3 'Did you say the stars were worlds, Tess?'

4 'I hope it is a chance for earning money. It is no other kind of chance'

5 'I want you to whistle to my bullfinches'

Identify the person 'to whom' this comment refers.

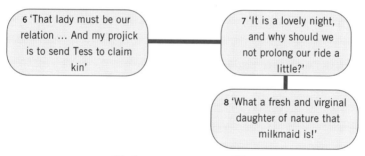

6 'That lady must be our relation ... And my projick is to send Tess to claim kin'

7 'It is a lovely night, and why should we not prolong our ride a little?'

8 'What a fresh and virginal daughter of nature that milkmaid is!'

Check your answers on page 76.

B *Consider these issues.*

a How Tess responds to the news of her noble ancestors.

b How Hardy presents the village people at the club-dance and at Rolliver's.

c The character of Alec d'Urberville and his behaviour towards Tess.

d The changing seasons and their connection with the story.

e Joan Durbeyfield in comparison with Tess.

f Hardy's presentation of religion in Chapter 14.

g How Talbothays is shown as a pleasant environment.

h How Angel Clare views Tess.

CHAPTERS 25–44
PHASE THE FOURTH – 'THE CONSEQUENCE'

CHAPTERS 25–7 (ANGEL CONSULTS HIS PARENTS)

Angel's father is kindly but is set in his opinions.

Angel is confused about his relationship with Tess and feels he has a great responsibility to her now that he has awakened her affections. He goes to visit his family and we see how far apart he has grown from them in attitudes and ideas.

Alec's shadow is never far away throughout the story.

In the evening, Angel brings up the subject of marriage and Tess. His parents had hoped that he would marry Mercy Chant, a clergyman's daughter. However, they agree to meet Tess. His father rides with him part of the way when he returns to Talbothays and during the journey tells Angel how, one day, when he was preaching, he was insulted by Alec d'Urberville.

Angel has felt restricted at home.

When Angel reaches the dairy he finds that Tess has been resting. He meets her when she gets up for the afternoon skimming and he asks her to marry him. She admits that she loves him but says she cannot marry him. When pressed, she lies to him that it is because of the difference in their social class. Later in their conversation, Angel mentions his father's experience with Alec d'Urberville. This makes Tess more determined not to marry Angel.

COMMENT   We see Angel's home is governed by strict rules of religion, unlike the more natural environment of Talbothays.

His brothers are seen to be conventional and limited products of their upbringing and education.

When we see something of Angel's background we can understand a little of the way he behaves later in the story.

Tess loves Angel but fears that she will only bring shame on him if she marries him.

GLOSSARY

noctambulist night walker

Walt Whitman American poet (1819–92)

pachydermatous thick-skinned like an elephant

mead an alcoholic drink made from honey

Antinomianism a belief that faith in Christ is the highest moral law

court-patched seventeenth- and eighteenth-century ladies wore small patches on their faces, like imitation moles

Wycliff, Huss, Luther, Calvin leading figures of Protestantism

Christiad, Pauliad writings about Christ and St Paul

Schopenhauer, Leopardi philosophers

Correggio, Velasquez painters

Diocesan Synod an assembly of clergy

dapes inemptae (Latin) home-produced food

delirium tremens (Latin) shaking madness brought on by heavy drinking

Pauline view view according to St Paul

fibrils small fibres

Tractarian High Church movement

Pantheistic finding God in all things

CHAPTERS 28–30 (TESS FINALLY ACCEPTS)

Angel does not believe that Tess's refusal is final and he continues to ask her why she will not marry him. She promises to give him a reason on the following Sunday and meanwhile she begins to see that she will eventually accept him even though she fears the consequences.

The country people have a broad sense of humour.

On Sunday morning dairyman Crick tells of a man who was tricked into marriage. All the company find this funny except Tess. When she meets Angel, she tells him she will not marry him for his sake. Angel is puzzled but does not give up hope.

PHASE THE FOURTH – 'THE CONSEQUENCE'

Angel remembers seeing Tess at the club-dance at Marlott.

One afternoon, Angel volunteers to drive the milk to the station and persuades Tess to go with him. As it gets darker it begins to rain. On the way back Tess attempts to tell Angel about her past but she is hindered by his interruptions and reassurances and eventually she loses her courage and gives up. At last she agrees to marry him.

COMMENT   We share Tess's discomfort at dairyman Crick's story. She feels it has elements of her own situation. She would be tricking Angel if she did not tell him about her past.

On the journey to the station and back we are reminded of several threads of Tess's story: they pass the ruin of an old d'Urberville manor; the stars are a reminder of Tess's conversation with her brother on the night their horse was killed; and Angel's cautious driving and his consideration for Tess are a contrast to Alec's behaviour.

Tess displays her lack of education by thinking that centurions live in London. Angel makes gentle fun of her.

Hardy maintains tension by the way in which Tess's attempts to tell about her past are constantly frustrated.

GLOSSARY   trowing believing
'sigh gratis' to sigh without hope of reward (from *Hamlet*)
carking worrying, being anxious
cust (dialect) cursed
scram (dialect) puny, weak
Caroline of the time of Charles I and Charles II
centurions Roman military leaders
lucubrations studies or thoughts carried on late at night

CHAPTERS 31–2 (NAMING THE DAY)

Tess's mother has an easy-going approach to morality.

Tess writes to her mother who answers her and advises her not to tell Angel about Alec and the baby. Tess decides to accept this advice. The autumn spent in the company of Angel is a period of great happiness for Tess. Angel presses her to set a date for their wedding and she becomes nervous again. When Mr and Mrs Crick and two of the dairymaids surprise them together, Angel announces that they are to be married.

The other girls cannot bring themselves to resent Tess's good fortune. Tess herself feels that they are purer than she is and that Angel should have married one of them.

Tess regrets leaving Talbothays. This has been the happiest period of her life.

By November Tess has still not named a wedding date. Angel will soon be leaving the farm and dairyman Crick has said that he will not be needing female help for much longer so Tess agrees to be married on 31 December. After the marriage they are to stay at Wellbridge in a house which once belonged to the old d'Urbervilles. Angel wishes to study the working of a flour mill there.

Pathetically, Tess wants to believe that her mother is right. This is not in keeping with her own sense of right and wrong.

COMMENT

We see that the love between Angel and Tess is in danger of being too idealistic and detached from reality, although Tess can feel the troubles from her past waiting like wolves out in the darkness.

Tess's goodness is highlighted by the inability of the other girls to resent or dislike her for winning Angel.

PHASE THE FOURTH – 'THE CONSEQUENCE'

GLOSSARY　　　　J an old form of I

Byronic than Shelleyan referring to the Romantic poets

champaign open level countryside

springe (old English) a trap

dogs fire irons, supports for logs

baily bailiff, farm manager

bolting sifting flour

CHAPTERS 33–4 (MARRIAGE AND CONFESSION)

Tess realises she cannot escape her past unless they move hundreds of miles away.

When they visit the nearest town Tess is insulted by a man who recognises her from the time she was working on the d'Urberville estate. Angel knocks the man down and later has a nightmare about the incident. Once again Tess feels that she should not be getting married. She decides to write the truth about her past and to put the note under Angel's door. In the morning, Angel's manner towards her is as affectionate as ever and she cannot tell whether he has read her note or not.

On the morning of the wedding day the lovers find that the dairyman has had the kitchen decorated in their honour. None of their relatives are coming to the wedding: Tess's owing to the distance, Angel's because they disapprove of his hasty marriage to a dairymaid. Angel is hurt by his family's attitude but thinks they may be impressed by Tess's noble ancestry.

Curious about her note, Tess goes to Angel's room and discovers it still there, hidden under the carpet. She destroys it.

The legend of the d'Urberville coach is mentioned.

Once more she tries to confess to Angel before the wedding but he overrules her. After the wedding they set off from the dairy in a state of great happiness. As they are leaving, a cock crows three times. This is considered to be a bad omen.

At Wellbridge Tess is startled by two unpleasant portraits of female d'Urberville ancestors. Angel thinks of his responsibilities towards Tess's future wellbeing.

Their luggage is late in arriving but a parcel is delivered which contains some of Angel's family's jewels which are to be the property of his wife during her lifetime. When the luggage arrives we hear that one of the dairymaids has got drunk and another has tried to drown herself.

Angel confesses to some immoral behaviour when he was younger and living in London. Tess takes this opportunity to tell him about her own past.

COMMENT   Tess is unnerved by the incident with the Tantridge man and would like to delay the wedding.

Mislaid letters are a favourtie device of Hardy's.   Twice more her good intentions are frustrated when her note goes under the carpet and when Angel will not listen to her confession on their wedding morning.

After the wedding Tess fears that Angel loves some image of her and not her real self.

When Angel confesses about his past indiscretion, Tess feels relieved at the chance to unburden herself.

GLOSSARY   **drachm**   a very small weight

blower   a cover above a fireplace to increase the draught

randy   a noisy party

partie carrée   (French) party of four

Friar Laurence   character in *Romeo and Juliet*

gallied   (dialect) frightened

withy-bed   an area of willows

good trencher woman   woman with a good appetite

traps   personal belongings

night-rail   (dialect) nightdress

Integer vitae   (Latin) wholeness of life

PHASE THE FIFTH – 'THE WOMAN PAYS'

CHAPTERS 35–7 (PARTING)

Tess knew that Angel had married some idealised version of her.

Angel cannot believe her at first. He breaks out into **ironic** (see Literary Terms) laughter and then he tells her she is not the woman he thought he was marrying. He does not respond to her pleas. She promises to do anything he wishes. When he goes out for a walk she follows him. He admits that what happened to her was not her fault, but he cannot come to terms with it. He even suggests it has some connection in his mind with the corrupt aristocracy she is descended from. Tess offers to kill herself to relieve him of the burden but he dismisses this as foolishness. He tells her to go to bed and they spend the night in separate rooms.

Next day Angel asks her if the man she was involved with is still alive. When she answers 'yes', it seems to affect Angel deeply. For several days he goes to study the workings of the mill. He then tells Tess he will not divorce her but they will have to part and she agrees to go home.

Angel will wish later that Tess had told him about the sleep-walking incident.

In the night Angel enters Tess's room, sleep-walking. He picks her up and kisses her, treating her as if she were dead. He carries her across a river by a dangerous bridge and for a moment she thinks he is going to drown her. Finally he lays her in an empty stone coffin in the grounds of an abbey. She takes him back to his bed and in the morning he is unaware of what has happened.

Angel persists with his plan and they call at Talbothays dairy on their way. They agree to pretend that all is well between them and afterwards they reach the place where they are to part. Angel gives Tess money and says that he will let her know where he is when he is settled and that he may come to fetch her, but she must not attempt to go to him. He says that she may write if she is ill or in need. They then part and Angel watches until her carriage disappears over a hill.

COMMENT   We feel Tess's distress at Angel's response to her confession all the more because she has been so innocently happy to make it.

We can see an element of Victorian double standards in Angel's reaction. It was regarded as somehow worse for a woman to have lapsed morally than for a man to have done the same.

Tess puts herself entirely at Angel's mercy. This is most strongly demonstrated in the sleep-walking incident when she does not care if he drowns her in the river.

Angel is redeemed a little in our eyes when he tries to ensure that Tess is provided for while he attempts to come to a decision about their future.

GLOSSARY   **prestidigitation** sleight-of-hand, conjuring trick

good-hussif (dialect) needlework bag

Agape (Greek) love feast

tester canopy

dimity stout cotton cloth

M. Sully-Prudhomme French poet (1839–97), given to writing highly emotional poetry

boreal Northern

CHAPTERS 38–40 (SEPARATE WAYS)

Tess's parents are unsympathetic and selfish.   When Tess arrives home she tells her mother what has happened. Her mother calls her a fool for telling Angel the truth and is worried how Tess's father will take the news as he has been boasting about the marriage at the pub.

She feels that there is no longer room for her at home and when she has a letter from Angel she uses it as an

excuse for leaving. She gives her mother half of the
money Angel has given her.

Angel returns to his parents' home blaming himself for
having married into the sort of decayed aristocratic
family which he had always despised. He intends to
emigrate to Brazil and thinks he will eventually send for
Tess to join him. He lies to his parents as to the reason
he is on his own and he also lies to them when
questioned about Tess's character. He feels some
resentment against Tess for having put him in this
position.

*Izz Huett is
tempted by Angel's
offer but is honest
about Tess's love.*

Calling at Wellbridge to pay some rent he owed, Angel
meets Izz Huett, one of the dairymaids who loved
him. He gives her a lift in the direction she is going and
he tells her that he and Tess have parted. He asks
Izz if she will go with him to Brazil but, when she
reminds him of how much Tess loved him, he changes
his mind. He is tempted to drive over to Tess's
parents' home but stops himself with the argument
that nothing has changed. That night he leaves for
Brazil.

COMMENT   Tess speaks in **dialect** (see Literary Terms) when she is
at her parents' home.

We see that Angel's parents have narrow and
conventional views. They are unhappy about Angel
going to a Roman Catholic country.

Angel is tormented by his father's reading from the
Bible about the value of a virtuous woman.

Hardy takes sides and, at the end of Chapter 39,
comments on Angel's limited and mistaken views.

Angel's uncharacteristic offer to Izz Huett shows the
strain he is under as does his indecision about going to
see Tess at Marlott.

GLOSSARY   **'Nation** an oath, short for damnation

unceiled without a ceiling

glane (dialect) sneer

Weirtz, Van Beers painters

Pagan moralist Roman Emperor Marcus Aurelius

the Nazarene Jesus

CHAPTERS 41–4 (THE FIELDWOMAN)

Tess spends the summer working at a distant dairy and finds harvest work in the autumn. She sends her mother some of her money to repair the roof of the family home and as winter approaches she is becoming hard up.

Angel's sufferings make us feel more sympathetic towards him.

We hear that Angel is suffering hardship in Brazil and that opportunities there are not as he expected.

Tess is like a hunted animal herself.

Marian, one of the dairymaids, has told Tess of some work and she is on her way to join her when she meets the man who was knocked down by Angel for insulting her. She runs into a wood to escape from him and she spends the night there, although she is disturbed by strange noises. In the morning she discovers a number of pheasants which have been wounded by hunters and she puts them out of their misery.

Tess decides to dress as plainly as possible to avoid the unwanted attentions of men. She makes her way from farm to farm until she reaches Flintcomb-Ash where Marian is working. She hides the fact that she is married and is employed by the farmer's wife, beginning hard work on the land.

Marian and Tess work in the fields, digging and cutting swedes. When it snows they work indoors at reed-drawing which is even harder. They are joined at the farm by Izz Huett and the three women reminisce about the good days at Talbothays.

PHASE THE FIFTH – 'THE WOMAN PAYS'

When Tess eventually meets the farmer he turns out to be the man whom Angel hit and who had frightened her on the road. He demands an apology but she refuses although she knows he will make life hard for her. Marian tells Tess of Angel's offer to take Izz to Brazil. Tess is upset and feels she ought to write to Angel, but she is unable to finish the letter.

Angel's brothers show little Christian charity when they discuss his marriage.

Tess decides to go to Angel's parents to find out if there is any news of him. She sets off walking early one Sunday morning but as she nears Emminster, where they live, she loses confidence. She hides her boots in a hedge and puts on her light shoes. There is no-one at home when she reaches the vicarage and she walks past the church as the congregation is coming out. Angel's two brothers are walking behind her and they meet Mercy Chant. They talk about their brother's unfortunate marriage, then one of them finds Tess's boots which are taken to be given to the poor.

Feeling humiliated, Tess returns to Flintcomb-Ash. On the way she hears a man preaching to some villagers in a barn and, recognising the voice, she looks in to find that the preacher is Alec d'Urberville.

COMMENT

Tess's pride will not allow her to contact Angel's parents and she does not want her own parents to know of her continued separation from her husband. She feels this will reflect badly on Angel.

The wounded birds symbolise Tess's own suffering.

The condition of the wounded birds reminds her that her own suffering is only to do with society's artificial rules.

The bare and bleak countryside at Flintcomb-Ash is in keeping with the dreary and harsh circumstances of Tess's life.

When she recognises the farmer it is further proof that she cannot escape her past.

Hardy poignantly shows us the barrier between the social classes in Tess's experience when she tries to visit Angel's parents.

GLOSSARY

éclat (French) brilliant effect

mommet (dialect) scarecrow

Cybele goddess of nature

clipsed or colled hugged or pestered

lanchets, lynchets beds of flint

integument skin, rind

terraqueous of both earth and water

reed-drawing preparing straw for thatching

thirtover (dialect) cross or contrary

lackaday (dialect) careless

crape-quilling a closely pleated material

guindée (French) stiff, proper

ranter unofficial preacher, often wild and emotional in style

antinomian a belief that Christians are released from the obligation of 'observing' the moral law

A Identify the speaker.

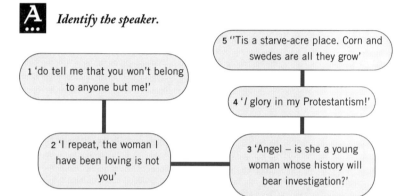

5 "'Tis a starve-acre place. Corn and swedes are all they grow'

1 'do tell me that you won't belong to anyone but me!'

4 'I glory in my Protestantism!'

2 'I repeat, the woman I have been loving is not you'

3 'Angel – is she a young woman whose history will bear investigation?'

Identify the person 'to whom' this comment refers.

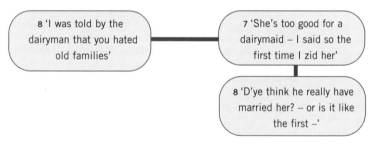

8 'I was told by the dairyman that you hated old families'

7 'She's too good for a dairymaid – I said so the first time I zid her'

8 'D'ye think he really have married her? – or is it like the first –'

Check your answers on page 76.

B Consider these issues.

a Tess's attempts to tell Angel about her past.

b The attitudes of Angel's parents and his brothers towards his marriage.

c The dangers of over-idealised love as presented in this section.

d The way Hardy uses unfortunate incidents, unpleasant details and bad omens to build up an atmosphere of doom.

e The credibility and effectiveness of Angel's sleep-walking.

f How Hardy presents the characters of Izz, Marian and Retty.

g How Tess's pride contributes to her sufferings.

h How Hardy presents the harshness of life at Flintcomb-Ash.

CHAPTERS 45–59
PHASE THE SIXTH – 'THE CONVERT'

CHAPTERS 45–7 (TESS IS PURSUED BY ALEC)

Alec selfishly blames Tess for tempting him.

Alec has been converted by Angel's father. He is shocked to see Tess and he follows her. She is angry with him and has only contempt for his conversion and his beliefs. He makes her swear on a stone cross that she will not tempt him. She later finds that the place has evil associations.

Several days later Alec approaches her when she is working in the field and asks her to marry him. She refuses and reluctantly tells him she is married. She tries to write to Angel again but does not finish the letter.

One day Alec arrives when she is alone at her lodgings. He says he is unable to stop thinking about her and that she should pray for him. He says that she tempts him away from his religion. Tess argues with him, using some of the ideas that she has learned from Angel.

The hardships of Tess's family are used by Alec to put pressure on Tess.

In March Tess is working, feeding wheat to a threshing machine. Alec comes and watches her. He is no longer dressed as a preacher. When she stops for lunch he tells her that he has given up preaching and he wants her to go to live with him and he will help Tess's family. He says he has been convinced against religion by Angel Clare's arguments which were quoted by Tess. She strikes him across the face but he says he will return for her answer later.

COMMENT   It is **ironic** (see Literary Terms) that Alec has been converted to religion by the Reverend Clare and that he should abandon his new-found faith through the arguments of Angel as related by Tess.

PHASE THE SIXTH – 'THE CONVERT'

As with her frustrated attempts to confess to Angel, Hardy maintains tension with Tess's unfinished attempts to write to her husband.

The relentless demands of the threshing machine are contrasted with the old slow hand methods. Agriculture is changing and becoming dehumanised. The machine minder is a stranger and stands apart from the workers.

GLOSSARY   *bizarrerie* (French) oddness

Paulinism as in the teachings of St Paul

Cyprian image image of Venus, goddess of love

Methodist a Christian church which was formed by people who left the Church of England

wuld (dialect) old

petite mort (French) faintness

Dictionnaire Philosophique a work by Voltaire (1694–1778)

primum mobile (Latin) first mover, creator of the world

Tophet (biblical) a place of fire

Plutonic of Pluto, the god of hell

autochthonous native

stooded (dialect) stuck

hagrode hag-ridden, bewitched

Weltlust (German) delight in the world

bachelor-apostle Luke

skimmer-cake a kind of dumpling or pudding

CHAPTERS 48–50 (CRISIS AT HOME)

The exhausting work continues into the evening. Alec returns and waits for Tess to finish. He walks with her to her lodgings and again offers to help her family. She almost agrees but then tells him she wants nothing from him, for them or herself.

Tess finally writes to Angel.   Tess sits down and writes a long letter to Angel, begging him to save her from what threatens her.

Angel's parents forward the letter to Brazil. They are concerned about him and hope that he will return soon. Angel himself has been having fresh thoughts about his behaviour towards Tess and is beginning to appreciate her true worth.

Tess's young sister 'Liza-Lu comes looking for her with the news that her mother is very ill. She puts 'Liza-Lu to bed and sets off for home, leaving instructions for her sister to follow her the next day.

Alec shows his temper when Tess refuses his help again. Through the night Tess walks the fifteen miles to Marlott where she is soon involved in looking after the family and organising the planting of vegetables. One evening as she is working late on the family plot of ground she is approached by Alec who is dressed in a labourer's smock. He offers help again but she rejects him. She goes home to find that her father has died suddenly. This means that the family will lose their home as the lease ends with him.

COMMENT

Tess's letter is quite well written and we know that she has had some education, but she does include some **dialect** (see Literary Terms) phrases.

Angel's hardships in Brazil seem to have given him a broader outlook on life.

Just as we think Tess is safe for a while, another problem arises. Her father's death and the impending homelessness of her family make her more vulnerable to Alec's pressure.

GLOSSARY

'nammet-time' refreshment break
Pandemonium city of devils in John Milton's *Paradise Lost*
Hellenic Paganism the religion of the ancient Greeks
drave to toil
pricked and ducked tested for witches by sticking pins in them
or ducking them in water

Phase the sixth – 'the convert'

'whickered' sniggered or giggled

Other One the devil

'liviers' tenants who held the lease as long as they lived

Olympians important people like the gods who lived on Mount Olympus

Chapters 51–2 (HOMELESS)

Tess does not tell her mother of Alec's offer in case she is persuaded to accept.

As Old Lady Day approaches, the family prepares to leave the house. Tess feels that they might have been allowed to stay, had it not been for her bad reputation in the village. Alec comes and offers to let them live in the old poultry house at Trantridge but Tess refuses and tells him they have reserved accommodation at Kingsbere. In despair she writes an angry letter to Angel accusing him of cruelty.

She begins to think that, in a physical sense, Alec is her husband.

Alec, lying on the tomb of a genuine d'Urberville, is a symbol of the new rich having replaced the old landed gentry.

The family leave the house and travel to Kingsbere, meeting Izz and Marian on the way. When they are approaching Kingsbere they find that their rooms have been let to another family. Unable to find any alternative they have their goods unloaded at the churchyard and take shelter among the tombs of the d'Urbervilles. Inside the church Tess comes upon Alec lying on one of the tombs. She rejects him again but wishes she were dead and buried in one of the vaults.

Izz and Marian have been concerned about Tess and, a month later, when they hear that Angel is returning from Brazil, they write to him to warn him that she is in danger.

COMMENT   Independent peasant families like the Durbeyfields are gradually disappearing from the countryside as their leases run out. They are replaced by hired workers.

Some people in the village have disapproved of the family's morals since Tess's pregnancy. We see Hardy's rejection of narrow-minded prejudices.

It is a measure of Tess's desperation that she writes to Angel in such a resentful way.

It is extremely **ironic** (see Literary Terms) that the destitute Durbeyfields should have to take shelter among the tombs of their noble ancestors. This could be criticised as being too theatrical a representation of their downfall and decay.

The selfless actions of Izz and Marian and their concern for Tess are very touching.

GLOSSARY   **Old Lady-Day** the day when contracts begin and end in the countryside

huckster pedlar or hawker

the hexagon to the bee reference to the six-sided cells in a honeycomb

deparked converted from the grounds of a large manor house

stale urinate

tole (dialect) entice or tempt

PHASE THE SEVENTH – 'FULFILMENT'

CHAPTERS $53-56$ (REUNION AND MURDER)

Angel returns to his parents' house. His parents are shocked at the changes in him brought about by illness and hardship. He reads Tess's second letter and writes to Marlott to prepare her for his return. He receives a reply from Tess's mother and realises that they have moved, but he is not told where Tess is living. As he is setting out to search for Tess, Angel receives the note from Izz and Marian.

Angel's travels in search of Tess maintain the suspense.

Angel tries to trace Tess at Flintcomb-Ash, Marlott and Kingsbere. He eventually finds Mrs Durbeyfield who reluctantly tells him that Tess is living in Sandbourne, a large seaside resort.

With no other information than this, Angel goes to Sandbourne and begins to look for Tess. Next morning he finds out from a postman that someone called d'Urberville is staying at a certain boarding house. Angel assumes that Tess must be using her family's original name and he hurries to the address.

Angel notices that Tess's hands are pale and delicate now.

When she meets him she tells him it is too late. Alec has won her back through kindness to her family although she hates him for having told her that Angel would never return. She tells Angel to go. Angel blames himself for what has happened.

The blood-stain on the ceiling, like an ace of hearts, is symbolic (see Literary Terms) of love and gambling.

The landlady at the boarding house eavesdrops on Tess when she returns to her rooms and hears her accusing Alec of having destroyed her life. She then hears some angry words from Alec and there is some movement which makes her move away from the door. Later she observes Tess leaving the house. When she sees blood dripping through the ceiling she calls in a workman who finds Alec dead in bed. He has been stabbed.

COMMENT

The effects of his illness make us sympathetic towards Angel.

Hardy has kept us in suspense. Like Angel, we do not know where Tess is.

Sandbourne with its promenades and boarding houses is a very different environment from the countryside where Tess belongs. It is a place of fashionable idleness, suggesting decadence.

The murder of Alec is left to our imaginations as it is viewed through the experiences of the landlady.

GLOSSARY   **Crivelli's dead** *Christus* a painting of Christ
Faustina, Cornelia, Lucretia, Phryne virtuous and immoral women from Greek and Roman history

wife of Uriah (biblical) Bathsheba

Ixonian wheel (Greek mythology) Ixion was tied to a fiery wheel in Hell

wafer small wax seal on a letter

CHAPTERS 57–9 (A LITTLE TIME TOGETHER)

Angel is about to catch a train but he decides to walk on to the next station. On the way he is overtaken by Tess who tells him she has murdered Alec. He does not really believe this and thinks that she may have attempted to do it, but he is determined to take care of her. They wander without any real plan and take refuge in an empty house.

Even the caretaker is impressed by the innocence of the sleeping couple.

A week passes and Tess is reluctant to leave the house, but the caretaker finds them sleeping. They feel that there may be someone about so they leave and journey on until, that night, they discover they have arrived at Stonehenge. Tess begs Angel to allow her to rest there and she lies down on a stone slab. He fears that the place is rather exposed to view. Tess tells Angel that if anything should happen to her she wants him to marry her sister 'Liza-Lu. As dawn is breaking the police arrive and Angel asks them to wait until Tess has finished her sleep before arresting her.

PHASE THE SIXTH – 'THE CONVERT'

Tess is thinking of On a July morning Angel and 'Liza-Lu leave the city of
Angel's welfare Wintoncester on foot. They are near the top of a hill
when she asks him when they hear the clocks strike eight. A few minutes
to marry 'Liza-Lu. later they see a black flag being raised above the jail.
This is the signal that an execution has been carried
out. Tess has been hanged. In a while Angel and
'Liza-Lu walk on hand in hand.

COMMENT   Hardy lets us hope that there may be a chance of escape
with references to reaching London or Southampton,
but there is an air of doom about their wanderings.

Tess's final resting place before she is taken is **symbolic**
(see Literary Terms). She is like a pagan sacrifice on the
altar at Stonehenge. The 'pure woman' of Hardy's subtitle is the victim of an unscrupulous man, Alec, and
the narrowness and hypocrisy of conventional morality.

In the final chapter, Hardy treats the scene with a calm
detachment. We view the events from a distance which
suggests that we are helpless observers of events over
which we have no control, just like the couple who
watch the flag being raised over the jail.

GLOSSARY   **Antinous** a handsome youth who was a favourite of the Roman
Emperor Hadrian
Apollo god of the sun, an ideal of male beauty
Atalanta's race in Greek legend she would only marry a man
who could beat her in a race
trilithon two upright stones supporting a third laid across the
top
reared alerted, stirred up
Giotto Italian painter (1267–1337)
Gothic a medieval style of architecture
Aeschylean of the Greek playwright Aeschylus (Hardy is
referring to the idea that we are merely the playthings of the
gods)

A Identify the speaker.

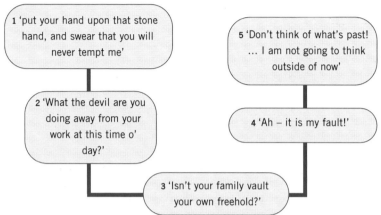

1 'put your hand upon that stone hand, and swear that you will never tempt me'

5 'Don't think of what's past! ... I am not going to think outside of now'

2 'What the devil are you doing away from your work at this time o' day?'

4 'Ah – it is my fault!'

3 'Isn't your family vault your own freehold?'

Identify the person 'to whom' this comment refers.

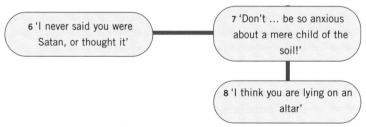

6 'I never said you were Satan, or thought it'

7 'Don't ... be so anxious about a mere child of the soil!'

8 'I think you are lying on an altar'

Check your answers on page 76.

B Consider these issues.

a Alec d'Urberville's religious conversion.

b Hardy's description of the steam threshing machine and its minder.

c How Angel has changed after his experiences in Brazil.

d Hardy's description of Sandbourne.

e The effectiveness of Hardy's account of the murder as seen through the experiences of the landlady.

f How satisfactory an ending you consider the final chapter to be.

PART THREE

COMMENTARY

THEMES

FATE

We are conscious that the lives of Hardy's characters are subject to forces and events beyond their control. Chance and coincidence bring about disasters and the characters have to deal with events in the best way they can.

The country people in his novels are often fatalistic about what happens to them and believe in omens and bad luck. Tess's mother typifies this view. After scolding Tess for not having pressed Alec to marry her when she is pregnant, she says, 'Well, we must make the best of it, I suppose. 'Tis nater, after all, and what do please God!' (Chapter 12).

Pride and idealism can bring unhappiness. Sometimes the fate lies in the characters' own natures. Tess's pride and her concern for Angel's reputation after he has left her prevent her from seeking help at an early stage of her troubles. Angel's uncompromising morality and his unrealistic ideal of womanhood prevent him from accepting and appreciating the real Tess.

Hardy suggests that we are at the mercy of an indifferent fate. After Tess is hanged, Hardy says that the gods have now finished their sport with her. Like all of us she was subject to the whim and mercy of whatever it is that controls events.

NATURE & THE SEASONS

We find the natural surroundings and the stages of the seasons are often in keeping with the events of the novel which borders on the **pathetic fallacy** (see Literary Terms). The story opens in spring and we see Tess at the May club-dance; it is late autumn when she returns pregnant from Tantridge. The Valley of the Great Dairies is describes as being like a land of milk and honey and it is during this summer that Tess is happiest. Her sufferings at Flintcomb-Ash, a bleak place at the best of seasons, take place in winter.

Hardy shows how people's surroundings can have a profound effect on them.

It is in the heat of late summer, that Angel's passion overcomes him and he embraces Tess for the first time. 'Amid the oozing fatness and warm ferments of the Var Vale, at a season when the rush of juices could almost be heard below the hiss of fertilization, it was impossible that the most fanciful love should not grow passionate' (Chapter 24).

At other times it is made clear that nature is indifferent to the doings of mere mortals. When Angel and 'Liza-Lu are leaving Wintoncester, their heads bowed in grief, 'the sun's rays smiled on pitilessly'. Nature may affect our moods and behaviour, but we do not have any influence over nature.

RELIGION & MORALITY

Hardy said that his subtitle, 'A Pure Woman', caused more debate than anything else in the novel. The conventional morality of his time was such that a woman or girl who gave birth to a child out of wedlock could only be described as 'fallen', 'sullied' or 'ruined', and would not be a suitable wife for a respectable man. Hardy knew that it was commonplace for poor girls in service to be seduced or raped by their wealthy employers and then to be paid off to cope with their disgrace as best they could. Polite society chose to believe that this sort of thing was very rare and that poorer people had different moral standards anyway.

The double standards in the behaviour expected
from men and women is highlighted in the inability of
Angel to accept that Tess's past was no worse than his
own.

*Hypocrisy, cant
and bigotry are in
evidence.*

The Christian religion is presented in a poor light in
the novel, from the narrow-minded bigotry of the man
with the pot of paint, to the intolerance and snobbery
of Angel's brothers and Mercy Chant. The parson in
Marlott has not the Christian charity to give Tess's
dead baby a decent burial. Angel's father, although a
kindly and tolerant man, is too greatly concerned with
points of doctrine. Alec's brief period as an evangelist
demonstrates the shallowness of some forms of religious
enthusiasm. Tess's own faith is shown to be simple and
sincere as when she baptises baby Sorrow.

DECLINE OF THE PEASANTRY

Tess's family represents the small independent traders,
craftsmen and others who formed a rural population
above the level of farm labourers. In the novel we see
how precarious their position was becoming. An
accident, such as the death of the Durbeyfields' horse,
could threaten ruin. Common land enclosures had
taken away some of their opportunities to raise their
own livestock and large-scale farmers were keen to buy

*The Durbeyfields'
decline is typical of
the history of many
peasant families.*

up their smallholdings. As with the Durbeyfields, life-
tenancies were not renewed.

Tess's experience in employment is perhaps typical of
many members of this class, going into service in the
houses of the New Rich, wage-work on the large-scale
farms, travelling the country for work, moving to towns
or emigrating. Hardy regretted the loss of these people
as he felt that they were the keepers of the traditions
and folklore of rural England.

	Tess	The Changing Seasons	Changes in Agriculture
Phase I	**The Maiden**		
	The club-dance – Tantridge – rape/seduction by Alec	Spring to Autumn	Peasantry have precarious independence – e.g. death of horse spells ruin. Members of family may go into service like Tess
Phase II	**Maiden no More**		
	Tess pregnant by Alec – death of Sorrow – decides to leave home	Summer at harvest Spring when she leaves	New Rich buying estates – setting up as country gentry
Phase III	**The Rally**		
	Happy time working at Talbothays – meets and is attracted to Angel	Summer to Winter	Large-scale business farming – Talbothays a benevolent example
Phase IV	**The Consequence**		
	Hesitantly moves towards marriage – the confession	Winter when Angel leaves her	Even at Talbothays, work only seasonal
Phase V	**The Woman Pays**		
	Rejected by Angel – Flintcomb-Ash – return of Alec	Winter at Flintcomb-Ash	Women cheap labour
Phase VI	**The Convert**		
	Pursued by Alec – increased hardship – family homeless	Winter to Spring	Industrial farming – workers dominated by machine – peasantry disappearing from villages
Phase VII	**Fulfilment**		
	Angel returns – Alec murdered – Tess is hanged	Spring – Angel returns Summer – Tess executed	Some rural workers move to towns – perhaps involving degradation. Some emigrate

STRUCTURE

The story in its original form was written for serialisation in a magazine, which obviously had some influence on its structure. Hardy would have tried to include some interesting or exciting event in each episode. The complete novel appeared in book form in 1891 and Hardy reworked it and included material which the magazine editor had made him remove as unfit for family reading.

There is an obvious structure in the Phases, as Hardy called the parts which divide the book, and each phase ends with a crucial event or turning point in Tess's life.

The titles of the Phases remind us that this is Tess's story.

Tess's relationships with Alec and Angel also provide a structure. They are opposites but both bring suffering to Tess. During Angel's courtship of her, Alec remains in our consciousness like a threatening presence. His past actions destroy Tess's chance of happiness with Angel. When he returns in the flesh, there is a connection with Angel as he has been converted by Mr Clare. **Ironically** (see Literary Terms) Angel's arguments as related by Tess convince him to drop religion. During Alec's pursuit of Tess, the absent Angel is constantly brought to mind as we hear of his troubles and as Tess attempts to write to him.

Seasons and journeys are important elements in the structure.

Nature and the seasons also provide structure. The Valley of the Great Dairies is a pleasant and gentle environment where Tess spends several happy months. Flintcomb-Ash is bleak and exposed. The rape or seduction takes place in The Chase, a wild and ancient hunting forest. We see Tess set out hopefully in the spring on more than one occasion, her unhappy experiences are in the autumn or winter.

There are a series of journeys which help the structure, the most significant ones being when Tess leaves her home to find work, at Tantridge, Talbothays and Flintcomb-Ash, and her return from these places.

There are other journeys including the final wandering with Angel which leads to Stonehenge. These all mark significant stages in her life.

CHARACTERS

TESS DURBEYFIELD

Tess is central to the novel. It is her tale. No matter what happens to her she maintains her position as 'a pure woman' because of her honesty and integrity. Her goodness and generosity shine out of her. The dairymaids at Talbothays are unable to resent her success with Angel even though they are heartbroken.

She has had some education and we can see that she is somehow finer than her parents though not sophisticated or pretentious. She speaks in **dialect** (see Literary Terms) at home, but uses a more standard English in other situations.

Sensual yet pure

Passive but responsible

Honest and generous, naïve

Her beauty is both fresh and sensual, prompting different responses from different men. Angel idealises her as innocent and virginal. Alec lusts after her and accuses her of being a temptress. At times she finds this beauty a terrible burden and wishes she could escape her body. Later she says she only values her looks because they belong to Angel.

Tess takes great responsibilities on her shoulders. She takes the job at the d'Urbervilles because she feels responsible for the death of her family's horse. She supports her family whenever she can and eventually gives in to Alec because of the help he gives them. She even believes that their homelessness is due to her bad reputation in the village. She feels responsible for Angel's reputation when he has left her, and this along with her pride prevents her from seeking help from his parents.

Tess's pride and her courage are shown in her experiences at Flintcomb-Ash and her repeated refusal to accept Alec's offers. She wants nothing for herself. She only weakens when her family is destitute.

Another element of her character is her acceptance of fate and her passivity in certain situations, such as her agreement to do whatever Angel wishes when he has rejected her and, finally, when she is arrested at Stonehenge. '"I am ready," she said quietly' (Chapter 58).

ALEC D'URBERVILLE

Handsome and nouveau riche

Has obsessive need to dominate

Tess's seducer has some of the qualities of the Victorian stage villain with his dark moustache, his full lips and his melodramatic phrases, such as, 'my beauty,' and, 'you'll be civil yet!'

He is a false d'Urberville as his family have only recently assumed the name, and this is not the only false thing about him. Like the devil, he appears in the story in various disguises, the dashing young rake, the evangelist preacher and one evening while Tess is burning weeds, he appears through the smoke carrying a pitchfork.

His pursuit of Tess is initially cynical and lustful. He wants power over her just as he has over his horse. Later he appears genuinely to care for her, though this is combined with an obsessive need to dominate and possess her. He represents an animalistic side to love whereas Angel represents the spiritual.

Although he is absent for a large part of the novel, he remains a threatening presence as when we hear of him insulting Mr Clare and when the man from Tantridge recognises Tess and refers to her association with him.

His desire for Tess causes him quickly to abandon his new-found religion. When she is at Flintcomb-Ash and later at Marlott and Kingsbere, he is relentless as he tries to wear down Tess's resistance and he cruelly taunts her with her husband's absence.

ANGEL CLARE

Idealistic and priggish

Angel has rejected the religious views of his parents and relies rather too much on his intellect. He feels that he is a freethinker but we discover that he is limited by his own idealism. He has a romanticised view of Tess from the start, seeing her as a perfect product of a natural and unspoiled environment. 'What a fresh and virginal daughter of Nature that milkmaid is!' he says to himself in Chapter 18. He brushes aside her attempts to correct this unrealistic picture and he is unable to deal with the truth when faced with it. 'You were one person; now you are another' (Chapter 35).

We feel that his treatment of Tess, after she confesses, is weak and priggish, although the sleep-walking scene suggests his inner turmoil. By the time he realises his mistake and comes to recognise Tess's true character and qualities it is too late. He does regain some credibility and some sympathy after his hardships in Brazil and we can hope for Tess's sake that he will find her and win her back. But things have gone too far and, in Chapter 53, he accepts blame: 'Ah – it is my fault!'

His care of Tess in their last few days together is touching and although the ending has been criticised as unrealistic or sentimental, it can be said to represent the idea that life goes on and that by encouraging the liaison between Angel and 'Liza-Lu, Tess will have helped her sister and her husband and salvaged something from her own defeat.

JOHN DURBEYFIELD

'Sir John', as he begins to call himself when parson Tringham informs him of his pedigree, is a rather feckless small trader and carrier. He has a heart complaint and a habit of drinking more beer than is good for him. It is because of his drinking that Tess has to take the horse on the night it is killed. He takes a pathetic and at times laughable pride in his noble ancestry and decides he cannot let down his good name by taking labouring work. He has little consideration for Tess as he is so wrapped up in his own vanity. Towards the end we have reports of his boasting and the state of his health. We hear of his death secondhand.

Feckless and vain

JOAN DURBEYFIELD

Tess's mother is a simple and rather careless peasant woman. She is superstitious and fatalistic, taking what comes. Her highest aspirations for Tess are that she should catch a rich husband and she fails to give Tess proper advice in how to deal with such as Alec. Hardy says there is a gap of 200 years between Joan with her oral peasant culture and her daughter who has been educated at the local National School.

THE REVEREND MR AND MRS CLARE

The Clares are genuine devout Christians. They are basically generous people who are limited by the conventions of their class and by the dogmas of their religious tendency. Mr Clare is obviously a brave man and in his preaching he exposes himself to verbal and even physical abuse. Tess, had she persevered, might have found them sympathetic and helpful.

MINOR CHARACTERS

Dairyman Crick

Mr Crick is a solid, decent middle-aged man who manages the dairy in an efficient yet kindly way, sharing the work with the others. He has not yet cast off the old ways as he considers sending for a conjuror or wise-man when the butter will not set. He is good-humoured and full of stories, and, as an employer, provides a contrast with the bullying farmer Groby at Flintcomb-Ash.

Izzy, Marian and Retty

The three dairymaids provide a kind of background against which we and Angel can appreciate Tess's qualities. The girls are unable to grudge Tess her position in Angel's affections even though they are all in love with him too. They recognise that she is finer than they are. They add to the happy atmosphere at Talbothays. At one point Izz agrees to go to Brazil with Angel but he changes his mind. Both Izz and Marian are supportive of Tess at Flintcomb-Ash and later they write to Angel, warning him of Tess's plight.

Mrs d'Urberville

Alec's mother, a wealthy widow, is apparently aware of her son's bad character but she indulges him. Her blindness means she is unaware of Tess's beauty and does not recognise Alec's motive for bringing her to the house. Her hobby is rearing ornamental fowl and birds.

LANGUAGE & STYLE

Hardy's narrative style is one which uses different points of view at different times in the story. Sometimes he writes as though he is retelling a tale which has been handed down from people who observed some of the events or were themselves told about them. When Angel and Tess are walking at night after Tess's confession, a local man sees them and it is said that he remembered this incident a long while after. When Hardy begins to tell us about Angel Clare, it is as though he has had to piece him together from vague descriptions. 'Angel Clare rises out of the past not altogether as a distinct figure' (Chapter 18).

Hardy's use of different viewpoints helps to give the story credibility.

Sometimes Hardy likes to show us a scene as experienced by one of the characters, an outsider perhaps, who does not realise the full significance of what is being observed, for example, the landlady who eavesdrops on the quarrel between Tess and Alec and who is alerted by the bloodstain, and the caretaker who finds Angel and Tess asleep in the empty house.

Hardy also lets us see events through the eyes of some of the main characters and in this way we become involved in their emotions and identify strongly with them.

At other times Hardy observes in a detached way, describing a scene or a piece of countryside before gradually moving in to focus on a character or characters within the scene and at last moving the story along through action and dialogue. A good example of this is Chapter 24 when he describes the effects of the late summer heat before moving in on one particular hot day when Angel is watching Tess milking. His characters are often figures in a landscape, dwarfed by the broad expanses of countryside. Tess and Marian at Flintcomb-Ash are described as being like two flies crawling on the surface of the field.

Hardy uses dialect very effectively in portraying country people.

Hardy's use of **dialect** (see Literary Terms) for the conversation of the country people is always convincing. He has a good ear for the speech rhythms of the people he came from. Occasionally his dialogue can be a little stiff in moments of high drama. Some of the conversation between Angel and Tess at the boarding house in Sandbourne suffers in this way. Alec d'Urberville's stage-villain phrases in the early part of the book almost make him a caricature: 'Well, my beauty', 'you artful hussy' (Chapters 5 and 8).

Hardy was one of the few writers who was successful both as a poet and as a novelist. We can see his poetic abilities in his powers of description and his use of **imagery** (see Literary Terms). In Chapter 30 he uses effective **metaphors** and **similes** (see Literary Terms) to describe the change of light and the appearance of the water's surface as rain begins to fall in the evening, 'The quicksilvery glaze on the rivers and pools vanished: from broad mirrors of light they changed to lustreless sheets of lead, with a surface like a rasp ... Remote Egdon disappeared by degrees behind the liquid gauze.' The **assonance** and **alliteration** (see Literary Terms) and the rhythms in the following passage are almost hypnotic in their evocation of the season of fruitfulness. 'Amid the oozing fatness and warm ferments of the Var Vale, at a season when the rush of juices could almost be heard below the hiss of fertilization, it was impossible that the most fanciful love should not grow passionate' (Chapter 24).

Hardy's poetic skills are evident in his descriptive language.

PART FOUR

STUDY SKILLS

HOW TO USE QUOTATIONS

One of the secrets of success in writing essays is the way you use quotations. There are five basic principles:

- Put inverted commas at the beginning and end of the quotation
- Write the quotation exactly as it appears in the orginal
- Do not use a quotation that repeats what you have just written
- Use the quotation so that it fits into your sentence
- Keep the quotation as short as possible

Quotations should be used to develop the line of thought in your essays.

Your comment should not duplicate what is in your quotation. For example:

> **Tess begs Angel to forgive her after she has confessed about her past. 'In the name of our love, forgive me!' she whispered with a dry mouth. 'I have forgiven you for the same!'**

Far more effective is to write:

> **Tess, after her confession, begs Angel for forgiveness. 'I have forgiven you the same!' she whispers.**

The most sophisticated way of using the writer's words is to embed them into your sentence:

> **Tess, after her confession, begs Angel's forgiveness, in the name of their love. She has forgiven him, 'for the same!'**

When you use quotations in this way, you are demonstrating the ability to use text as evidence to support your ideas – not simply including words from the original to prove you have read it.

Everyone writes differently. Work through the suggestions given here and adapt the advice to suit your own style and interests. This will improve your essay-writing skills and allow your personal voice to emerge.

The following points indicate in ascending order the skills of essay writing:

- Picking out one or two facts about the story and adding the odd detail
- Writing about the text by retelling the story
- Retelling the story and adding a quotation here and there
- Organising an answer which explains what is happening in the text and giving quotations to support what you write

- Writing in such a way as to show that you have thought about the intentions of the writer of the text and that you understand the techniques used
- Writing at some length, giving your viewpoint on the text and commenting by picking out details to support your views
- Looking at the text as a work of art, demonstrating clear critical judgement and explaining to the reader of your essay how the enjoyment of the text is assisted by literary devices, linguistic effects and psychological insights; showing how the text relates to the time when it was written

The dotted line above represents the division between lower- and higher-level grades. Higher-level performance begins when you start to consider your response as a reader of the text. The highest level is reached when you offer an enthusiastic personal response and show how this piece of literature is a product of its time.

Coursework
essay

Set aside an hour or so at the start of your work to plan what you have to do.

- List all the points you feel are needed to cover the task. Collect page references of information and quotations that will support what you have to say. A helpful tool is the highlighter pen: this saves painstaking copying and enables you to target precisely what you want to use.
- Focus on what you consider to be the main points of the essay. Try to sum up your argument in a single sentence, which could be the closing sentence of your essay. Depending on the essay title, it could be a statement about a character: Our first impression of Alec d'Urberville is of a young man with, 'an almost swarthy complexion, with full lips, badly moulded'. He has a forceful and confident manner; an opinion about setting: The countryside of Wessex in its various aspects has a great influence on the mood and feeling of different stages of the novel; or a judgement on a theme: Journeys are an important theme in the story. Tess's journeys mark significant stages in her tragic life.
- Make a short essay plan. Use the first paragraph to introduce the argument you wish to make. In the following paragraphs develop this argument with details, examples and other possible points of view. Sum up your argument in the last paragraph. Check you have answered the question.
- Write the essay, remembering all the time the central point you are making.
- On completion, go back over what you have written to eliminate careless errors and improve expression. Read it aloud to yourself, or, if you are feeling more confident, to a relative or friend.

If you can, try to type your essay, using a word processor. This will allow you to correct and improve your writing without spoiling its appearance.

Examination
essay

The essay written in an examination often carries more marks than the coursework essay even though it is written under considerable time pressure.

In the revision period build up notes on various aspects of the text you are using. Fortunately, in acquiring this set of York Notes on *Tess of the d'Urbervilles*, you have made a prudent beginning! York Notes are set out to give you vital information and help you to construct your personal overview of the text.

Make notes with appropriate quotations about the key issues of the set text. Go into the examination knowing your text and having a clear set of opinions about it.

In most English Literature examinations, you can take in copies of your set books. This is an enormous advantage although it may lull you into a false sense of security. Beware! There is simply not enough time in an examination to read the book from scratch.

In the
examination

- Read the question paper carefully and remind yourself what you have to do.
- Look at the questions on your set texts to select the one that most interests you and mentally work out the points you wish to stress.
- Remind yourself of the time available and how you are going to use it.
- Briefly map out a short plan in note form that will keep your writing on track and illustrate the key argument you want to make.
- Then set about writing it.
- When you have finished, check through to eliminate errors.

To summarise, • **Know the text**
these are keys • **Have a clear understanding of and opinions on the storyline,**
to success   **characters, setting, themes and writer's concerns**
             • **Select the right material**
             • **Plan and write a clear response, continually bearing the question in mind**

SAMPLE ESSAY PLAN

A typical essay question on *Tess of the d'Urbervilles* is followed by a sample essay plan in note form. This represents merely one form of approach to the answer. Do not be afraid to use your own ideas, or leave out some of those in the sample. Remember that quotations are essential to prove and illustrate the points you make.

In what ways does Hardy deal with change in the rural way of life in *Tess of the d'Urbervilles*?

Introduction   We are shown several different aspects of country life in the novel: different types of farming; changes in methods, customs and attitudes; many are reflected in the experiences of Tess and her family.

Part 1   Tess's father, an independent if inefficient dealer, a peasant; precarious living; death of the horse is a catastrophe; his illness and death bring poverty and homelessness to the family.

Part 2   Joan Durbeyfield, a peasant woman, uneducated, superstitious, a fund of custom and ballads; contrast with Tess who has had some education; Hardy says there is a gap of 200 years between them.

Part 3   The d'Urbervilles represent the New Rich, giving nothing to the rural economy; estates are just for show; Mrs d'Urberville's ornamental fowls are **symbolic** (see Literary Terms); taking names and trappings of old landed gentry; exploiting as Alec exploits Tess.

Part 4   Changes in farming: large-scale production; Talbothays a positive example; Flintcomb-Ash an unfavourable one; movement of workers; seasonal contracts; loss of village stability and traditions.

Part 5   Machinery and railways which increase commercial potential bring pressure on the workers; tyranny of threshing machine at Flintcomb-Ash; milk has to be at station in time for train; upsetting old natural rhythms of country life.

Part 6   End of the peasantry illustrated in the fate of Tess's family: end of lease with father's death; homeless like many such families; replaced by tied wage-workers living in property owned by their employers.

Conclusion   Through Tess's travels to find work to help support her family and her experiences Hardy shows us the changes in rural England and decline of the peasants; Tess's own tragedy and her fate **symbolic** of this decline.

FURTHER QUESTIONS

Make a plan as shown above and attempt these questions.

1 To what extent is Tess to blame for her own tragedy?

2 Compare and contrast the ways in which Angel and Alec affect Tess's life.

3 How effective is Hardy in presenting the country characters in the novel?

4 Discuss Hardy's skill in creating mood through the use of Nature.

5 How is Hardy's interest in history evident in the novel?

6 How far do you agree with Hardy's subtitle 'A Pure Woman'?

7 After reading the novel, what do you think are Hardy's views on religion?

8 Discuss the importance of journeys in the story.

9 Does Angel Clare deserve Tess's love?

10 Some of the events in the novel depend on coincidence or 'fate'. Discuss some of these coincidences and the effects they have on the story.

11 Examine how Hardy describes a scene through the eyes of one of the characters and comment on the effectiveness of this technique.

12 What does the novel tell us about the position of women in Victorian England?

PART FIVE

CULTURAL CONNECTIONS

BROADER PERSPECTIVES

You may find some of the following works helpful when you are studying *Tess of the d'Urbervilles.*

FILM

Roman Polanski's film, *Tess* (1979), which won awards for photography and design, is beautiful and faithful in its settings and its treatment of the story, although events are not described in the order of the novel and much of the novel is omitted.

ITV are producing a new adaptation of *Tess* in 1998.

Far from the Madding Crowd (1967) is a screen adaptation of another of Hardy's Wessex novels. The central character is again a woman, Bathsheba Everdene, who is pursued by three men.

WRITTEN WORKS

'Tess's Lament' is a poem by Thomas Hardy in which the narrator is Tess herself, lamenting her lost happiness.

'The Ruined Maid' is another poem by Hardy in which he takes a more **satirical** (see Literary Terms) approach to the 'ruin' of a country girl.

It would be helpful to read any of Hardy's other Wessex novels, particularly *Far from the Madding Crowd* and *Under the Greenwood Tree*, which have central female characters and which deal with life in the countryside which he loved so much.

A Taste of Honey (1958) is a play by Shelagh Delaney and tells of a teenage girl's coming to terms with her pregnancy and her loveless home in a northern town.

Possession by A.S. Byatt (1991, Vintage) is a modern novel which is partly set in Victorian times and deals with religious and moral constraints in conflict with passionate love.

A Preface to Hardy (1976, Longman) by Merryn Williams is a very informative and useful guide to Hardy's life and times and to his writings.

alliteration the same consonant repeated for rhythmical or sound effect

assonance the same vowel sound repeated for sound effect

caricature a likeness which is so exaggerated or distorted that it appears ridiculous

dialect a local or regional version of a language

imagery word pictures, descriptions and comparisons which conjure up a picture

irony saying one thing while meaning another; a situation or occurrence that has an importance which is not seen by the person involved

metaphor where a comparison is suggested by giving one thing the qualities of another

narrator the storyteller

pathetic fallacy a situation in fiction where nature, particularly the weather, seems to be in sympathy with human affairs

satire a piece of writing which criticises someone or something, through ridicule, usually humorously

simile making a comparison using, 'like', 'as', or 'as if'

stereotype a standard, fixed idea of a character, a 'stock' character, often ordinary or commonplace

symbol where one thing represents something else

TEST ANSWERS

GCSE and equivalent levels (£3.50 each)

Maya Angelou
I Know Why the Caged Bird Sings

Jane Austen
Pride and Prejudice

Harold Brighouse
Hobson's Choice

Charlotte Brontë
Jane Eyre

Emily Brontë
Wuthering Heights

Charles Dickens
David Copperfield

Charles Dickens
Great Expectations

Charles Dickens
Hard Times

George Eliot
Silas Marner

William Golding
Lord of the Flies

Willis Hall
The Long, the Short and the Tall

Thomas Hardy
Far from the Madding Crowd

Thomas Hardy
The Mayor of Casterbridge

Thomas Hardy
Tess of the d'Urbervilles

L.P. Hartley
The Go-Between

Seamus Heaney
Selected Poems

Susan Hill
I'm the King of the Castle

Barry Hines
A Kestrel for a Knave

Louise Lawrence
Children of the Dust

Harper Lee
To Kill a Mockingbird

Laurie Lee
Cider with Rosie

Arthur Miller
A View from the Bridge

Arthur Miller
The Crucible

Robert O'Brien
Z for Zachariah

George Orwell
Animal Farm

J.B. Priestley
An Inspector Calls

Willy Russell
Educating Rita

Willy Russell
Our Day Out

J.D. Salinger
The Catcher in the Rye

William Shakespeare
Henry V

William Shakespeare
Julius Caesar

William Shakespeare
Macbeth

William Shakespeare
A Midsummer Night's Dream

William Shakespeare
The Merchant of Venice

William Shakespeare
Romeo and Juliet

William Shakespeare
The Tempest

William Shakespeare
Twelfth Night

George Bernard Shaw
Pygmalion

R.C. Sherriff
Journey's End

Rukshana Smith
Salt on the snow

John Steinbeck
Of Mice and Men

R.L. Stevenson
Dr Jekyll and Mr Hyde

Robert Swindells
Daz 4 Zoe

Mildred D. Taylor
Roll of Thunder, Hear My Cry

Mark Twain
The Adventures of Huckleberry Finn

James Watson
Talking in Whispers

A Choice of Poets

Nineteenth Century Short Stories

Poetry of the First World War

Six Women Poets

Advanced level (£3.99 each)

Margaret Atwood
The Handmaid's Tale

William Blake
Songs of Innocence and of Experience

Emily Brontë
Wuthering Heights

Geoffrey Chaucer
The Wife of Bath's Prologue and Tale

Joseph Conrad
Heart of Darkness

Charles Dickens
Great Expectations

F. Scott Fitzgerald
The Great Gatsby

Thomas Hardy
Tess of the d'Urbervilles

James Joyce
Dubliners

Arthur Miller
Death of a Salesman

William Shakespeare
Antony and Cleopatra

William Shakespeare
Hamlet

William Shakespeare
King Lear

William Shakespeare
The Merchant of Venice

William Shakespeare
Romeo and Juliet

William Shakespeare
The Tempest

Mary Shelley
Frankenstein

Alice Walker
The Color Purple

Tennessee Williams
A Streetcar Named Desire

Jane Austen
Emma

Jane Austen
Pride and Prejudice

Charlotte Brontë
Jane Eyre

Seamus Heaney
Selected Poems

William Shakespeare
Much Ado About Nothing

William Shakespeare
Othello

John Webster
The Duchess of Malfi

York Notes – the Ultimate Literature Guides

York Notes are recognised as the best literature study guides.
If you have enjoyed using this book and have found it useful, you
can now order others directly from us – simply follow the ordering
instructions below.

HOW TO ORDER

Decide which title(s) you require and then order in one of the following
ways:

Booksellers
All titles available from good bookstores.

By post
List the title(s) you require in the space provided overleaf,
select your method of payment, complete your name and
address details and return your completed order form and
payment to:

Addison Wesley Longman Ltd
PO BOX 88
Harlow
Essex CM19 5SR

By phone
Call our Customer Information Centre on 01279 623923 to
place your order, quoting mail number: HEYN1.

By fax
Complete the order form overleaf, ensuring you fill in your
name and address details and method of payment, and fax it
to us on 01279 414130.

By e-mail
E-mail your order to us on awlhe.orders@awl.co.uk listing
title(s) and quantity required and providing full name and
address details as requested overleaf. Please quote mail
number: HEYN1. Please do not send credit card details by
e-mail.

York Notes Order Form

Titles required:

Quantity	Title/ISBN	Price

Sub total _____

Please add £2.50 postage & packing _____

(*P & P is free for orders over £50*) _____

Total _____

Mail no: HEYN1

Your Name _____

Your Address _____

_____

Postcode _____   Telephone _____

Method of payment

☐ I enclose a cheque or a P/O for £_____ made payable to Addison Wesley Longman Ltd

☐ Please charge my Visa/Access/AMEX/Diners Club card
Number _____   Expiry Date _____
Signature _____   Date _____

(please ensure that the address given above is the same as for your credit card)

Prices and other details are correct at time of going to press but may change without notice. All orders are subject to status.

☐ *Please tick this box if you would like a complete listing of Longman Study Guides (suitable for GCSE and A-level students)*

York Press

Longman

Addison Wesley Longman